Moo Pa Buddhas in a Cave

PRAISE FOR *STORYSHARES*

"One of the brightest innovators and game-changers in the education industry."
– Forbes

"Your success in applying research-validated practices to promote literacy serves as a valuable model for other organizations seeking to create evidence-based literacy programs."

- Library of Congress

"We need powerful social and educational innovation, and Storyshares is breaking new ground. The organization addresses critical problems facing our students and teachers. I am excited about the strategies it brings to the collective work of making sure every student has an equal chance in life."
– Teach For America

"Around the world, this is one of the up-and-coming trailblazers changing the landscape of literacy and education."
- International Literacy Association

"It's the perfect idea. There's really nothing like this. I mean wow, this will be a wonderful experience for young people."   - Andrea Davis Pinkney, Executive Director, Scholastic

"Reading for meaning opens opportunities for a lifetime of learning. Providing emerging readers with engaging texts that are designed to offer both challenges and support for each individual will improve their lives for years to come. Storyshares is a wonderful start."
- David Rose, Co-founder of CAST & UDL

Moo Pa Buddhas in a Cave

Gajinder Kaur

STORYSHARES

Story Share, Inc.
New York. Boston. Philadelphia.

Moo Pa Buddhas in a Cave

Published in the United States by Story Share, Inc.

The characters and events in this book are fictitious. Any similarity to real persons, living or dead, is entirely coincidental.

Storyshares
Story Share, Inc.
24 N. Bryn Mawr Avenue #340
Bryn Mawr, PA 19010-3304
www.storyshares.org

Inspiring reading with a new kind of book.

Interest Level: Middle School
Grade Level Equivalent: 3.0

9798885977098

Book design by Storyshares

Printed in the United States of America

Storyshares Presents

1

The boys cycled excitedly to Tham Luang.

The newest members of the football team would write their names on the walls of the cave, leave handprints, and that would make them part of it forever

Moo Pa: the Wild Boars of Mae Sai.

Coach Ake was leading the twelve boys.

It was a dry day and the wind blew strongly from the green hills above.

They left their bikes and bags at the entrance of the cave and went in barefoot.

It was Night's 17th birthday. He was the eldest on his team.

His family waited for him to return so they could celebrate, (they had even bought a surprise SpongeBob cake.)

The boys had only about an hour to explore.

It was dark inside, but they had torches. They went in.

Outside, the wind brought in dark clouds over the jungle, and it started to rain.

It was at first just a drizzle, but then it became a downpour, with thunder and lightning.

Cold gusts of air drifted inside.

The boys were having fun, unaware.

Water dripped down the trees of the forests and mixed with the earth.

It gathered by and by, as it continued to rain even more.

Soon there was so much that a flood gushed into the cave, finding no other place to be.

2

Coach Ake heard the water come in strongly and told the boys, "Move in! Hurry!"

They ran deeper and deeper into the cave to find shelter, or else they might be swept away.

They searched for a dry spot away from the sweeping flood.

At last, further and deeper within, they found a mud ledge to squat on.

Perfect.

As soon as the water went back, they would leave, assured Coach Ake.

Meanwhile, all they could do was wait.

It was dark and quiet inside the cave. They couldn't hear a thing happening outside.

They kept their torches on.

And waited.

Coach Ake thought it wise to dig into the earth with the rocks around, so they could sit closer together.

It would keep them warm.

They shared all the food they had brought in.

And waited.

They drank water that dripped from the walls and rocks.

And waited.

The flood rose until it almost reached the ledge.

Coach Ake said, "No need to worry. They will come looking for us."

The Senior Coach of the team knew they were visiting Tham Luang today, so he would certainly send someone to find them as soon as the rain stopped.

Coach Ake looked at the boys.

They were getting restless. And afraid.

He remembered his practices in the monastery.

He had been a Buddhist monk before he became a football coach.

"Let us offer prayers," he said.

The team prayed together for help to come their way, and to return home safely to their families soon.

"Now, let us watch our breath. Breathe in, slowly. Watch. And breathe out slowly, and watch," he instructed.

The team listened to him eagerly, just like they did when he taught them football.

Yes, this would help keep the boys calm, safe, and together, thought Coach Ake.

They would use less air, lose less energy, and also not be so afraid anymore.

It became quieter, darker, and colder.

Not a sound echoed but the boys' breath.

They breathed in and breathed out, watching by the moment.

It became darker and darker, and all the torches went out, one by one.

But they waited.

And waited.

Soon, they began to feel weak without food.

"Try not to think about it," said Coach Ake.

But they couldn't help it. They were quite hungry.

As they tried not to think about it, they missed it even more.

Someone thought of stir-fried basil pork and rice. Someone thought of KFC. Someone missed ice cream and cakes.

They even thought of their parents being angry with them, for they were so very late.

They waited, because that was all they could do. They waited on the ledge for a very, very long time.

The water did not flow back.

Coach Ake kept practicing the breathing exercises with them.

Moment by moment passed in the darkness.

In the coldness.

In the dampness.

In the quietness.

There was only silence and breath.

3

Suddenly, they heard the water ripple.

They stopped — was the flood going back, finally?

Somebody came up and out of the water with a light. No, wait, there were two of them! Two divers!

They spoke English. Only Adul spoke English well on his team.

"How many of you?" shouted one of the divers with a shaky voice.

"Thirteen," replied Adul calmly.

"Thirteen! BRILLIANT!" The diver sounded quite relieved.

"Can we leave the cave now?" asked Adul. He didn't know what was going on outside.

"Yes. Many people are coming. You have been inside for ten days."

Ten days? The team had lost all track of time... they had only been breathing and waiting.

The divers were shocked to find them, let alone find them so calm and patient. That shock was mirrored by everyone outside Tham Luang, because all of Thailand, all the world, had been hoping and praying the boys would be found safe.

Finally, after ten days of searching, the divers from the UK had found them. They were brought food and fresh water, and a doctor came in to check on them. They were to be rescued by the divers, in groups of four. The boys were tied up to a diver each, who swam them through the muddy river.

Outside the cave, great crowds had gathered to see them safe and alive. Their families had come too.

The teammates were put on stretchers and taken to the hospital, where they stayed until the doctors said they were healthy and strong again.

It didn't stop raining that day and the cave flooded up even higher. But the boys had been rescued now. Coach Ake had kept their spirits up and and given them the strength to get through. He had made Little Buddhas of the Wild Boars, thanks to his breathing practice. He had kept them alive with it.

Moo Pa Buddhas in a cave. An adventure they would never forget all their lives.

About The Author

Gajinder Kaur is a contributing author to the Storyshares collection whose title, Moo Pa Buddhas in a Cave was a finalist in the 2022 Story of the Year contest.

About The Publisher

Story Shares is a nonprofit focused on supporting the millions of teens and adults who struggle with reading by creating a new shelf in the library specifically for them. The ever-growing collection features content that is compelling and culturally relevant for teens and adults, yet still readable at a range of lower reading levels.

Story Shares generates content by engaging deeply with writers, bringing together a community to create this new kind of book. With more intriguing and approachable stories to choose from, the teens and adults who have fallen behind are improving their skills and beginning to discover the joy of reading. For more information, visit storyshares.org.

Easy to Read. Hard to Put Down.

www.ingramcontent.com/pod-product-compliance
Lightning Source LLC
Chambersburg PA
CBHW071231170626
46809CB00005BA/2029